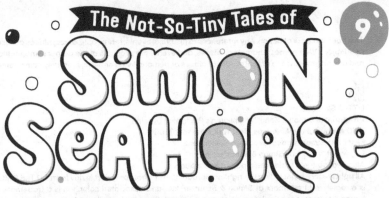

The Not-So-Tiny Tales of
Simon Seahorse

Climbing Mount Aquarius

By Cora Reef
Illustrated by Jake McDonald

LITTLE SIMON
New York   London   Toronto   Sydney   New Delhi

LITTLE SIMON

An imprint of Simon & Schuster Children's Publishing Division
1230 Avenue of the Americas, New York, New York 10020
First Little Simon hardcover edition November 2023
Copyright © 2023 by Simon & Schuster, Inc.
Also available in a Little Simon paperback edition.
All rights reserved, including the right of reproduction in whole or in part in any form. LITTLE SIMON is a registered trademark of Simon & Schuster, Inc., and associated colophon is a trademark of Simon & Schuster, Inc. For information about special discounts for bulk purchases, please contact Simon & Schuster Special Sales at 1-866-506-1949 or business@simonandschuster.com.
The Simon & Schuster Speakers Bureau can bring authors to your live event. For more information or to book an event contact the Simon & Schuster Speakers Bureau at 1-866-248-3049 or visit our website at www.simonspeakers.com.
Designed by Leslie Mechanic
The text of this book was set in Causten Round.
Manufactured in the United States of America 0923 LAK
10 9 8 7 6 5 4 3 2 1
This book has been cataloged with the Library of Congress.
ISBN 978-1-6659-2971-4 (hc)
ISBN 978-1-6659-2970-7 (pbk)
ISBN 978-1-6659-2972-1 (ebook)

Contents

Seahorse Storytelling

It was dinnertime at the Seahorse house, but everyone was so focused on the story being told that they'd barely touched their kelp spaghetti.

"Sir Sheldon knew that if he didn't make it to the top of Mount Aquarius by that evening, it would be too dark to continue."

"And then he'd have to go home?"
Simon Seahorse asked, his voice
hushed.

Simon's dad nodded.

Usually, *Simon* was the one who shared exciting tales with his eleven siblings during meals. Tonight, though, it was Mr. Seahorse's turn.

"Sir Sheldon decided that he had come too far to turn back," Mr. Seahorse went on. "As he neared the top of the mountain, it grew so dark that he could barely see his own claws! But suddenly, a magical glow lit his path. He spied a handwritten sign that said TO TOP, and he decided to trust whoever had made that sign, even though the little path wasn't on the map he was using. Well, it was a good thing he did, because Sir Sheldon scrambled the rest of the way to the summit. He'd done it! He'd reached the top of Mount Aquarius!"

Everyone cheered as Mr. Seahorse took a bow. Then, finally, they dug into their spaghetti, chatting excitedly.

"Wow, Simon," his oldest sister, Kya, said. "I didn't think anyone could tell stories as good as yours, but Dad's was amazing."

"Do you think it was true?" Simon asked.

"Mount Aquarius *is* a real place . . . but does it glow with magic?" Kya laughed. "I don't think so!"

Simon smiled. Even if his sister was right, it was fun to imagine that the story *could* be true. He couldn't wait to share it with his friends at school the next day—with a few fun twists of his own, of course.

By the time he met his best friend, Olive Octopus, at the corner of Seaweed Lane the next morning, Simon was about to burst with excitement.

SEAWEED LANE

"What's up, Simon?" Olive asked, a suspicious look on her face. "You seem even bouncier than usual."

"My dad told us the *best* story last night," he said. "I can't wait to share it with everyone."

Olive laughed. "Just try not to get *too* carried away this time."

"I know, I know," Simon said, but his mind was already spinning with ideas.

The two friends hopped onto the current that would bring them to school, and Olive took a notebook out of her bag. She began flipping through pages and pages of notes. "What's that?" Simon asked.

"Ideas for our bioluminescence project," Olive said. "There are so many cool things that make their own light! It's going to be hard to pick just one by Monday."

Simon gasped. Oh no! His head had been so full of stories that he'd forgotten about the project that was due in just a few days!

The End . . .
and More

When Simon and Olive arrived at Coral Grove Elementary, they spotted their friend Cam Crab scuttling along.

"Have you two been working on your bioluminescence projects?" he asked. "Mine is almost done."

"Oh, um, kind of," Simon mumbled back.

Cam shook his head. "Let me guess. You got caught up in a story."

"Something like that," Simon said with a laugh. "Speaking of stories, make sure to tell everyone to meet by the slide at recess. I have a fantastic new one to tell."

Cam rolled his eyes. "Whatever you say," he said. Cam could be crabby sometimes, but Simon knew Cam enjoyed his stories just as much as everyone else.

The morning dragged on as Simon waited impatiently for a good time to tell his friends about Sir Sheldon. He tried to focus on doing research for his project, but his mind kept drifting away.

Just before the bell rang for recess, Ms. Tuttle called Simon up to her desk. "You seem a little distracted, Simon," she said. "Have you chosen which sea creature you'd like to focus on for your bioluminescence project?"

"Not yet," Simon admitted.

"Well, I'm sure you'll pick something just right," Ms. Tuttle said with an encouraging smile.

Simon thanked her and then zipped out onto the playground as fast as his fins would carry him. His friends were already gathered at the slide, waiting for him.

"What's this new story you have for us?" Lionel asked as Simon swam up.

"Oh, it's a good one," Simon said. He launched into the story about Sir Sheldon and Mount Aquarius. As he went, he added a few new twists and turns to make it even more exciting. In Mr. Seahorse's tale, Sir Sheldon had *not* almost been swallowed up by a whale, but in Simon's story . . . it was a close call!

Simon was having so much fun making the story his own that he was barely even thinking when he came to the ending. "And that's why I'm going to climb Mount Aquarius this weekend, just like Sir Sheldon!" he announced.

There was a moment
of stunned silence.
"Wait," said Nix,
flicking her eel tail.
"*You're* going to
climb Mount Aquarius?"

Simon froze for a moment. Had he
really just said that?

"W-well– " he stammered.

Before Simon could explain that he'd gotten a little carried away, Lionel chimed in. "Wow, that's so cool, Simon!"

Everyone else looked impressed too. Everyone except Olive.

"Are you *really* going to climb all that way, Simon?" she asked.

Simon swallowed. He knew he should tell his friends that it was just part of the story. But somehow, he found himself saying, "Yes. Yes, I am."

The Right Time

That night, Simon tried to work on his bioluminescence project, but there were too many sea creatures to choose from. Glowing worms, snails, squid—how could he pick just one?

Simon finally decided he'd work on it more tomorrow. But his mind kept spinning, not with ideas but with worries.

Why had he told his friends that he was going to climb Mount Aquarius? Of course, it wasn't true. He'd never even *heard* of Mount Aquarius until his dad had mentioned it. Simon sometimes embellished the truth to make stories more exciting, but he'd never *lied* to his friends before. What was he going to do?

The next morning, Simon's stomach felt like it was tied in square knots.

"Simon, you've barely touched your scrambled kelp," Mr. Seahorse said. "You didn't find any of Sir Sheldon's old shells in there, did you?"

Simon tried to laugh at his dad's joke, but it came out like a sigh. Just hearing Sir Sheldon's name made Simon feel terrible all over again.

After breakfast, he hurried out of the house early and took the current to school alone. He needed to tell his friends the truth, but when? After lunch when everyone was full and happy? Or at recess, when they'd be busy playing on the playground?

When Simon arrived at school, he found his friends waiting for him by the entrance. Maybe he should just tell them now and get it over with.

But before he could say anything, Nix swam over. "Simon," she said, "I have something to say."

Simon swallowed. Had Nix figured out that he hadn't told the truth yesterday?

"We're sorry if it sounded like we didn't believe you about climbing Mount Aquarius," Nix went on. "We were just surprised. But if you want to climb it, then we support you!"

Simon blinked. "W-what?"

"And we can help you train!" Lionel jumped in.

"Here," said Cam. "This might help." He held out a book called *The Crab's Guide to Expert Climbing.*

"Wow, thanks, Cam," Simon said, taken aback.

Cam shrugged, like it was no big deal, but Simon was touched. If *Cam* was trying to support him, that said a lot.

The only one who hadn't spoken yet was Olive. Simon expected to see the same suspicious expression on her face as yesterday. But she gave him a bright smile.

"If you really want to climb Mount Aquarius, Simon," Olive said, "then we're happy to help."

Simon's chest filled with warmth. He couldn't believe how encouraging his friends were being! It didn't seem like the right time to tell them that he'd made the whole thing up.

Later, he decided. He'd do it later, for sure.

Getting
into Gear

At recess, Simon's friends couldn't wait to share their ideas about how he should prepare for his big climb.

"You should go down to the bubble ball fields and swim laps," Lionel suggested.

"I can set up an obstacle course for you to train on," Nix chimed in.

Olive tapped her chin, thinking. "I can do some research when I'm at the library tonight."

"I already gave Simon a book on climbing, remember?" Cam pointed out.

"Well, yes," Olive said gently. "But that was a climbing guide for *crabs*."

"Oh, I have a backpack you can borrow, Simon!" Lionel cried.

Simon couldn't believe how excited his friends were about him climbing Mount Aquarius—and how sure they seemed that he could actually do it. It made *him* think, too, that maybe he could do it.

But then Simon remembered that he hadn't even told his dad about the idea. How would Mr. Seahorse react?

"Simon," said Olive, pulling him out of his thoughts, "how about we go into town after school and get supplies for your climb?"

"Oh. Um, sure," Simon said.

So that afternoon, Simon and Olive took the current into town. Normally, the two of them would swing into Sandy's Candy Shop or the Kelpy Cone, but today they headed for the Coral Grove Natural Sea Market.

"This place has everything you'll need for your hike," Olive assured Simon.

They passed rows of organic kelp chips, kelp energy bites, and green tubes of seaweed gel. Then they found a section of ropes, helmets, and headlamps. Simon had no idea climbing mountains required so much gear!

"Hello! I'm Beanie," a jellyfish behind the counter called. "What can I do for you today?"

"This is Simon," Olive answered. "He's going to be climbing Mount Aquarius this weekend and needs some supplies."

Beanie's eyes widened. "You're climbing Mount Aquarius?"

Simon gulped. "I . . . yes, I am."

"Good for you!" she said. "Let me show you what you'll need."

Beanie led them through the market, pulling this and that off the shelves. "These will help keep up your energy for the long climb," she explained, grabbing some yummy-looking kelp chip bars.

Before Simon could ask if he could sample one of the bars now, Beanie added, "Will you be sleeping on the mountain or doing a day trip?"

Sleep on the mountain? In the dark? All alone? Simon gulped.

"A day trip," Olive answered for him.

Beanie piled everything on the counter. "You can take this all home now, Simon, and have your dad stop by next week to pay for it."

"Wait, you know my dad?" Simon asked.

"Of course!" said Beanie. "He's a loyal customer!" Then she hurried off to pack everything up.

Simon frowned. He had no idea his dad shopped here.

"This is great," Olive said as she helped Simon bring his new supplies back home. "You're all ready for your climb now!"

Simon managed a smile. "Great," he said, trying to sound excited. He was worried again, but this time for another reason. There was no chance Mr. Seahorse would actually let him climb the mountain . . . right?

Let's Train!

"I think it's a fantastic idea!" Mr. Seahorse said.

"You *do*?" Simon asked in disbelief. He'd waited until the very end of dinner to ask his dad about the climb, afraid he already knew the answer. But Simon had not been expecting *this*!

Simon's older brother Jet frowned. "Dad? Are you feeling okay?"

Mr. Seahorse laughed. "I'm fine. Why?"

"You're *really* going to let Simon climb Mount Aquarius?" Jet asked.

"I am," Mr. Seahorse said. "In fact, I have a headlamp you can borrow, Simon."

Simon was too stunned to answer.

As he swam off to bed that night, Simon realized that as fun as it had been to imagine himself climbing Mount Aquarius, part of him had been hoping his dad wouldn't actually let him do it.

Now Simon had no choice but to go through with the climb, no matter how scary it seemed. Unless he told his friends the truth. But ... was it already too late?

The next morning at school, Simon was so busy trying to choose an animal for his bioluminescence project that he didn't have a chance to talk to his friends.

When he got out to the playground at recess, Nix slithered over, beaming with excitement. "The new obstacle course is all ready for you!" she said, gesturing to a different part of the playground. "You can start training when you're ready."

"Oh, um . . . sounds great," Simon said. He and Nix swam over to the course.

A small crowd had gathered to watch. Simon was used to having an audience during bubble ball games, but the crowd still made him a little nervous.

"Let Simon's training begin!" Cam announced.

Simon sped through hoops, zipped along tunnels, and leaped over hurdles.

"Go, Simon! Go!" Nix cheered.

Then Simon practiced swimming up and down the lookout tower at the playground.

"Nice work, Simon," Lionel cried. "That's your fastest time yet!"

Finally, Olive sat him down and shared her research about Mount Aquarius.

"Mount Aquarius is the tallest mountain in Coral Grove," she began, before launching into a long, but surprisingly very interesting, presentation.

At the end of the day, Simon's fins were tired and his brain was bursting with information, but his heart was filled with hope. Maybe he really *could* climb the mountain after all.

Mount Aquarius

The next night, Simon couldn't fall asleep. In the morning, he'd be setting off for Mount Aquarius all on his own. He was both excited and terrified. And it didn't help that he *still* hadn't picked a sea creature for his school project!

Mr. Seahorse knocked on Simon's door. "Simon, you're still up?" he asked.

"I guess I'm a little nervous about tomorrow," Simon admitted.

"Well, I have something for you that might help," Mr. Seahorse said. He held out a glistening shell. "This is a special sundial seashell. It's said 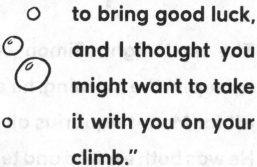 to bring good luck, and I thought you might want to take it with you on your climb."

Simon examined the shell, comforted by its sparkle and shimmer.

"Where did you get this?" he asked.

"Oh," his dad said with a flick of his fin, "I found it with an old friend." Then he tucked Simon into bed and said, "Now get some rest."

Simon closed his eyes, but it took a long time for him to drift off to sleep. And when he finally did, his dreams were filled with impossibly tall mountains.

The next morning, Simon swam down to the kitchen to find the table crowded with all his brothers and sisters.

"What's the occasion?" Simon asked. It was rare for everyone to gather together so early in the morning.

"We wanted to see you off!" Kya said, putting a bowl of kelp cereal in front of him.

"Oh! Thanks," Simon said. He tried to eat his breakfast, but his stomach was too full of nervous sea butterflies.

When it was time to leave, Mr. Seahorse helped Simon pull on his climbing backpack and headlamp.

Then he gave Simon a huge container of kelp chip cookies.

Simon laughed. "Dad, do you really think I can eat all of these?"

Mr. Seahorse smiled. "They're your favorite," he pointed out. "And they're good for sharing with friends." Then he gave Simon a hug and added, "Good luck today. I can't wait to hear all about it!"

Simon waved goodbye and opened the front door. He was surprised to find Olive waiting on the other side.

"What are you doing here?" he asked. "I thought we were going to meet at the current." Then Simon realized it wasn't just Olive—*all* his friends were there.

"We thought you might like some company on the way," Olive said.

Simon gave her a grateful smile as the group headed to the current that would bring them to Mount Aquarius.

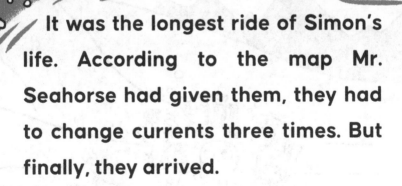

It was the longest ride of Simon's life. According to the map Mr. Seahorse had given them, they had to change currents three times. But finally, they arrived.

Simon held his backpack tightly as they swam through a field of seagrass toward the base of the mountain.

"Wow, there it is!" Lionel said when they came to a clearing.

Simon looked up . . . and up . . . and up. His stomach dropped. Mount Aquarius was taller and steeper than he ever could have imagined.

7

The Whole Truth

"Simon," Olive said, "are you okay?"

Simon wanted to say he was fine.
But when he opened his mouth, the
truth came pouring out instead.
"The thing is . . . I never planned to
climb Mount Aquarius," he said. "My
story about Sir Sheldon got away
from me and I couldn't take it back."

Simon looked at his friends. "I'm *so* sorry I lied to you all."

His friends looked back at him in surprised silence. Simon thought of how they'd helped and encouraged him the past few days, and it made him feel even worse.

Simon realized that there was only one thing to do.

"But I said I was going to climb the mountain, and I'm going to stick to my word," Simon went on. "Hopefully, I'll see you all back down here in a few hours."

Simon held his head high and began to swim toward the base of the mountain.

"Not so fast," Olive called, coming up beside him.

"What is it?" Simon asked. Then he stopped and glanced around at his friends. "Wait, why are you wearing backpacks?" Simon had been so nervous earlier that he must not have noticed them.

"Because," Lionel said, "we're coming with you!"

"You . . . *are?*"
Simon asked.

Olive nodded.
"I had a feeling
you *might* have
gotten slightly

carried away with your story about
Sir Sheldon," she explained. "But I
thought that if we all climbed Mount
Aquarius together, we could turn your
story into a reality."

Simon's heart
swelled. He gave
Olive the biggest
hug he could.

"Wow, okay," Simon said when he finally pulled away. "In that case, let's get going!" He took out the trail guide that Olive had found in her research, and the group set off.

The bottom of the mountain was covered in tall seagrass, which made the path hard to see.

"There will be less seagrass higher up," Olive informed everyone. "Then it will be easier to follow the trail."

The friends wound their way around a huge boulder that reminded Simon of a dolphin.

"Huh," said Simon. "My dad's story had a dolphin-shaped boulder in it too." But Kya had said Mr. Seahorse's story wasn't real. So it was probably just a coincidence.

They hadn't gone far before Cam announced that it was time for a snack break. "If I don't eat every hour, I get pretty crabby," he explained.

Simon and Olive glanced at each other. "Now *that's* saying something," Simon whispered.

As Simon took out the large container of kelp chip cookies, he remembered what his dad had said about sharing them with friends.

"Olive, did my dad know you'd all be coming with me?" Simon asked.

"Of course," Olive said with a smile. "Did you really think he'd let you climb a mountain all by yourself?"

Simon chuckled. "I *was* surprised that he agreed so easily."

As Simon put away the last of the cookies, he noticed the special shell his dad had given him.

"What's that?" Nix asked.

"My dad said it would bring me luck on my climb," Simon explained.

"Let's hope he's right," said Nix. "We still have a long way to go!"

A Familiar Sign

Their journey was going well until the group came to a fork in the trail. Neither path was marked.

"Which way do we go?" Lionel asked.

"The fork isn't on the trail guide," Olive said.

Simon shook his head. "Now what are we supposed to do?"

"I have an idea," Cam piped up. "We can use my shell compass."

"How will that help?" Nix asked.

"See how on the trail guide the path heads east?" Cam said. "All we have to do is figure out which of these two paths is heading in that direction."

Cam held out the compass, and the little arrow spun around. He turned toward one path. "Since the compass always points north, that means this path leads west," he said.

"Which means the other one goes east?" Olive asked.

Cam checked his compass and nodded. "That's right. We need to go this way."

"Wow. Thanks, Cam!" said Simon. "I don't know what I would have done if I'd been alone."

The group continued climbing and climbing. The seagrass was gone, and the mountain was rockier now, covered in beautiful bits of different-colored coral.

Every so often, the friends stopped to look at the view. It was amazing!

Less amazing was how far they still were from the top. Everyone was already pretty worn out. How were they ever going to make it to the top *and* back down again before dark?

Then Simon spotted something half-hidden in the nearby coral. It was a small sign with an arrow and the words TO TOP written on it.

Simon gasped.

"What is it, Simon?" Cam asked.

"That sign," he said. "My dad mentioned one just like it in his story about Sir Sheldon." Did that mean parts of Mr. Seahorse's story were real after all?

"It says here we should keep going along the main path," Cam said, glancing at the trail guide.

But Simon's heart was thumping with excitement. "I think we should follow the arrow," he said.

The others hesitated, but Simon was already swimming past the sign. "Come on!" he called. "This way!"

"Are you sure about this, Simon?" Olive asked, coming up beside him.

"This is just like from my dad's story," he said. "If I'm right, this is a shortcut that *will* take us to the top!"

The smaller trail was steep, but the friends kept going. They hiked around some coral and over a big rock. When they got to the other side, they were blown away by what they saw in front of them.

This certainly *felt* like the top of a mountain!

Suddenly a voice called out from behind them. "Hello? What are you doing up here?"

The Real
Sir Sheldon

Simon spun around to find a hermit crab scuttling over to them.

"W-we're just climbing to the top of Mount Aquarius," Simon said.

The hermit crab laughed. "Well, congratulations," he said. "You've made it! Let me introduce myself. I'm Sir Sheldon."

Simon's eyes went wide. "*You're* Sir Sheldon?" he said in disbelief. "You mean . . . you're *real*?"

The hermit crab laughed again. "Last time I checked. And you are?"

"I'm Simon Seahorse."

This time, Sir Sheldon raised his

eyebrows. "Hold on, are you Stan Seahorse's kid?" he asked.

"Yes, that's my dad! But how do you know him?" Simon said.

"Stan and I once climbed this very mountain together when we were young!" Sir Sheldon replied.

Simon was shocked. So the story his dad had told him ... it was *all* true? And Simon's dad knew it was true because ... he had been *in* it?

That explained why Beanie at the market had said Mr. Seahorse was a loyal customer. And why the dolphin-shaped boulder and the TO TOP sign in his dad's story were real.

After Simon introduced his friends, they were all really curious to hear the story of Sir Sheldon's climb. Sir Sheldon recounted the tale that Mr. Seahorse had told Simon. But this time, the story wasn't only about Sir Sheldon. It was about Sir Sheldon *and* Mr. Seahorse!

"Why didn't my dad tell me he'd climbed the mountain with you?" Simon asked when Sir Sheldon was done.

Sir Sheldon shrugged. "It was a long time ago. And Stan always liked making his stories big and exciting. Maybe it was more fun for him to tell it about someone else."

Suddenly, Simon saw something gleaming around Sir Sheldon's neck. It was a shell on a string. A very familiar-looking shell.

Simon quickly dug around in his backpack until he found the sparkling shell that his dad had given him the night before. He held it up beside Sir Sheldon's.

Sir Sheldon smiled. "Stan and I found these identical shells on our climb and decided they were lucky. I've been wearing mine ever since."

"That must be why my dad gave me his," said Simon. Then he frowned. "But wait. If you two climbed Mount Aquarius years ago, why are you still here?"

"When we made it to the top of the mountain, I loved it here so much that I decided to stay," Sir Sheldon explained. "Stan returned to Coral Grove, promising to visit from time to time."

Simon was amazed. His dad had probably climbed the mountain many times. He wanted to ask Sir Sheldon so many more questions, but Olive tapped him gently with an arm.

"Simon," she said, "it's getting kind of late. We might want to head back down before it gets too dark."

Sir Sheldon smiled. "One more thing before you go," he said. "The light show!"

Best Friends

"The light show?" Simon asked. Then, he remembered the "magic glow" from his dad's story, which had lit Sir Sheldon's path to the top of the mountain. Had that part of the story been true too?

"I suppose we can stay a *little* longer," Olive said. Simon could tell she was also curious.

Simon and his friends settled in beside Sir Sheldon. A moment later, they watched in awe as the water above them began to grow brighter. Then dozens of glowing sea stars began shooting past, lighting up the entire mountain.

Simon had never seen anything more beautiful!

"How are the sea stars glowing like that?" Nix whispered.

"I wonder if it's magic," Lionel whispered back.

But Simon quickly realized the answer. "They're bioluminescent!" he cried. And just like that, he knew exactly which creature he was going to pick for his school project.

When the light show was over, Simon and his friends thanked Sir Sheldon and promised to come back and visit soon.

"Make sure you give your dad a big hello from me," Sir Sheldon told Simon.

"Oh, don't worry," Simon said. "I'll fill him in on the whole story when I get home!"

After one last goodbye, the group started the journey back down the mountain.

Going downhill was much easier than going uphill, and soon Simon's mind began to drift. He still couldn't believe that his dad had once hiked up Mount Aquarius with his friend, Sir Sheldon. And now Simon had done the same with *his* own friends!

Olive swam up beside him. She didn't say anything, but she didn't need to.

Simon squeezed his dad's lucky shell and smiled at Olive. His stories sometimes got away from him, but they also led to many adventures, both real and imagined. Simon knew he was lucky to have his friends by his side through them all.

SIMON'S STORY

Mount Aquamarine was the tallest mountain in the entire ocean. And Sean Seahorse was going to climb it! The only problem was . . . Sean had never climbed a mountain before. Luckily, he had a group of best friends who agreed to help him. They had to start their climb in the middle of the night to make it to the top before the next night. Sea stars lit the path for them, and they began. But as they climbed, they unknowingly made a wrong turn. The path they were on led them right into a den. And that den belonged to . . . a giant squid! Sean and his friends were scared, but the squid turned out to be really friendly and she guided them back to the right path. After a few more hours of climbing, they made it to the top. It was the most beautiful view Sean had ever seen in his life. And it was even better because all his friends were with him.

THE END

**Simon Seahorse has
many more stories to tell!**

The Not-So-Tiny Tales of **SIMON SEAHORSE** — Simon Says

The Not-So-Tiny Tales of **SIMON SEAHORSE** — I Spy...a Shark!

The Not-So-Tiny Tales of **SIMON SEAHORSE** — Don't Pop the Bubble Ball!

The Not-So-Tiny Tales of **SIMON SEAHORSE** — Summer School of Fish

The Not-So-Tiny Tales of **SIMON SEAHORSE** — Into the Kelp Forest

The Not-So-Tiny Tales of **SIMON SEAHORSE** — Shell We Dance?

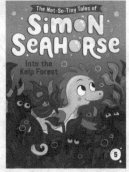

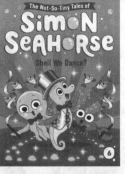

The Not-So-Tiny Tales of **SIMON SEAHORSE** — Dragon Dreams

The Not-So-Tiny Tales of **SIMON SEAHORSE** — Seas the Day!

The Not-So-Tiny Tales of **SIMON SEAHORSE** — Climbing Mount Aquarius

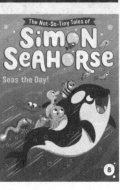
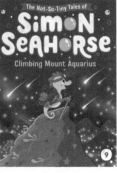

GOOD D🐾G

Hungry for adventure?